OLD MAN RABBIT'S
DINNER PARTY

His bag bumped against his back.

OLD MAN RABBIT'S DINNER PARTY

BY CAROLYN SHERWIN BAILEY

ILLUSTRATED BY ROBINSON

·NEW·YORK·
·THE·PLATT·&·MUNK·CO INC·

Man Rabbit had been exercising, and that was another reason why he was so warm.

He had started off early that morning, lippity, clippity, down the little brown path in front of his house that led to Farmer Dwyer's corn patch. The path was covered with snow but some red and yellow leaves still showed. Old Man Rabbit carried a big bag and he scuffled through the leaves.

OLD MAN RABBIT'S DINNER PARTY

Old Man Rabbit sat at the door of his little house. He was eating a nice, ripe turnip. It was a cold and frosty day, but Old Man Rabbit was all wrapped up round and round, with his best red woolen muffler. He did not mind if the wind blew through his whiskers and made his ears stand up. Old

In the corn patch he found some fat red ears of corn that Farmer Dwyer had left, so he dropped them into his bag. He found in the garden some purple turnips and yellow carrots and russet apples that Farmer Dwyer planned to store in his cellar. Old Man Rabbit squeezed under the big red barn door and filled the corners of his bag with potatoes.

He started off early that morning.

He also took a couple of eggs in his paws.
He might want to stir up a pudding for his
dinner.

Then Old Man Rabbit started home down
the little brown path. Every time his bag
bumped against his back, his mouth watered.
He went home by criss-cross rabbit ways, so
as not to meet any of his neighbors. He

He emptied his bag in his front room.

emptied his bag in his house and arranged the food in piles in his front room: The corn in one pile. The turnips and carrots in one pile. The potatoes in one pile. The apples in one pile. He beat up his eggs, added flour and lots of raisins for his pudding. He put his pudding in a bag and started it steaming over his little stove. Then he sat down

in his doorway, munching a carrot and thinking what a clever old man he was.

And while Old Man Rabbit, all wrapped up in his red muffler, and munching a carrot, sat there in front of his house, he heard a small sound in the fallen leaves. It was Billy Chipmunk going home to the old stone wall where he lived. Billy Chipmunk was hurry-

Old Man Rabbit sat in his doorway.

ing. He was blowing on his paws to keep them warm.

"Good morning, Billy Chipmunk," said Old Man Rabbit. "Why are you running so fast?"

"Because I am cold and hungry," said Billy Chipmunk. "It is going to be a hard winter. It is going to be a very cold and hard winter, with no apples left. All this morning

I have been looking for an apple. I have not found one."

Then Billy Chipmunk went chattering by, his fur standing up straight in the wind.

No sooner had he passed than Old Man Rabbit saw Molly Mouse scampering along the little brown path, her long gray tail rustling the leaves.

"Good morning, Molly Mouse," said Old

"Good morning, Molly Mouse," said Old Man Rabbit.

Man Rabbit. "Why are you scampering so fast?"

"I have been looking and looking for an ear of corn," Molly Mouse said in a sad chirping voice. "I am cold and hungry. The corn is all harvested. It is going to be a hard winter, a very cold and hard winter."

Then Molly Mouse went scampering by,

her long tail making a little gray line
through the leaves.

And soon after, Old Man Rabbit heard
another neighbor coming along. This time
it was Tommy Chickadee, hopping fast,
scolding *chick-chick-chick-a-dee* as he
went.

"Good morning, Tommy Chickadee," said
Old Man Rabbit. "What are you scolding
about?"

"What are you scolding about?" asked Old Man Rabbit.

"The weather and the bad times," chirped Tommy Chickadee. "Not a crumb of bread or a berry to be found anywhere." And Tommy Chickadee flew on, his feathers puffed out into a little gray ball.

Old Man Rabbit finished his carrot down to the leaves. He went into his house to put more wood into his stove and watch the

pudding boiling and bubbling in the pot. As it boiled it bumped against the pot and it smelled good. Old Man Rabbit looked into his front room at his corn, turnips, carrots, potatoes and apples, rubbing his stomach. But suddenly he had an idea.

It was a new idea for Old Man Rabbit. It caused him to scratch his head with his left

When the table was set, the pudding was done.

hind foot. It was an unusual idea, but it pleased him.

Old Man Rabbit took off his muffler and put on his large gingham apron. From a drawer he took his red-and-white checkered table cloth. He set his dining table with his best blue-banded dishes. When he had done this, the pudding was done. He lifted it, all steaming and good-smelling, from the pot,

turned it out of the bag and placed it in the middle of his table.

Around his pudding Old Man Rabbit heaped his ears of corn, his turnips, carrots, potatoes and apples. Then he found his big dinner bell, that was cracked and rusty for he had not used it in so long a time. He stood in his front door and rang his dinner bell loudly, *ding-dong, ding-dong-DING.*

He stood in his front door and rang the dinner bell.

He called loudly, "Dinner's on the table! Come to dinner everybody!"

They all came. They brought friends too. Tommy Chickadee brought Rusty Robin who had a broken wing and so must stay in the deep woods all winter. Billy Chipmunk brought Chatter-Chee, an old squirrel who had forgotten where he had buried his few

nuts. Molly Mouse brought her boy friend, a young gentleman field mouse. When they all dashed into Old Man Rabbit's house and saw the table with the steaming, good-smelling pudding, the corn, the turnips, the carrots, the potatoes and the apples, they forgot their table manners. They went right to eating, every one of them!

They almost forgot their table manners.

Old Man Rabbit was kept busy waiting on them. He gave the currants from the pudding to Tommy Chickadee and Rusty Robin. He selected the most tender turnips and carrots, and the best apples for the others. Old Man Rabbit was so busy that he had little time for eating, but he did not mind that. No, he did not mind that one

least little bit. It made him feel good inside
to see his neighbors eating.

Nothing was left when dinner was over.

Then Tommy Chickadee hopped onto the
table and chirped,

"Three cheers for Old Man Rabbit!"

Molly Mouse jumped up beside him and
chirped,

"Three cheers for Old Man Rabbit!"

"Three cheers for Old Man Rabbit's Dinner Party!"

"Hurray! Hurray!" they cheered in chirps and chatters and peeps.

Old Man Rabbit was so surprised that he did not get over it for a week. He had really and truly given a dinner party. Why was he surprised? Because dinner with his neighbors tasted better than if he had eaten alone.